BEOWULF

BEOWULF

WELWYN WILTON KATZ

ILLUSTRATED BY

LASZLO GAL

A GROUNDWOOD BOOK
DOUGLAS & McINTYRE
TORONTO VANCOUVER BUFFALO

GEAT ROYAL HOUSE

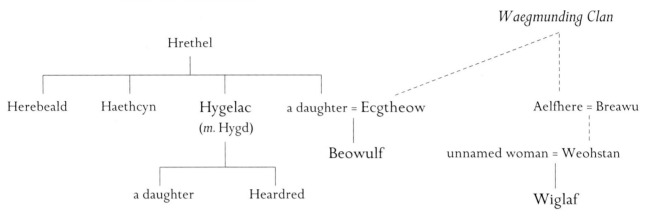

Waegmunding Clan

Hrethel

Herebeald   Haethcyn   Hygelac   a daughter = Ecgtheow   Aelfhere = Breawu
                          (*m.* Hygd)

                                                Beowulf   unnamed woman = Weohstan

         a daughter   Heardred   Wiglaf

DANISH ROYAL HOUSE

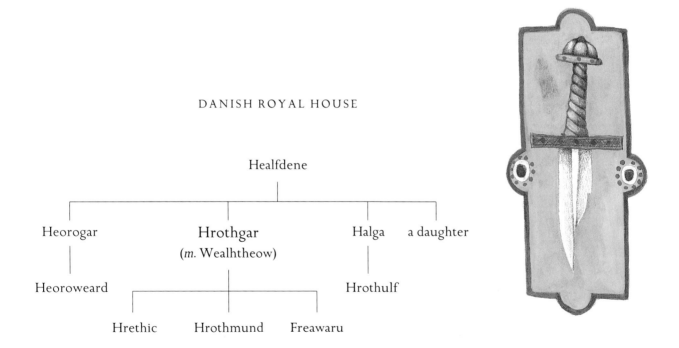

Healfdene

Heorogar   Hrothgar   Halga   a daughter
                (*m.* Wealhtheow)

Heoroweard   Hrothulf

         Hrethic   Hrothmund   Freawaru

DEEP NIGHT lay over the three small buildings of the last steading of the Waegmundings. Three buildings. Even so, it was too big, thought Aelfhere, Elder of Clan Waegmunding. His clan was dying out.

Aelfhere huddled over the glowing embers in the house's central hearth. For years there had been too few children. Now there was only one: his grandson, Wiglaf. The boy was sitting up, though it was much too late for him. He was playing on the sleeping bench with the latest of his foundling pets — a wolf pup.

Aelfhere could hear the laughter in Wiglaf's thoughts and had no heart to tell him to go to sleep. Too often there was horror in the boy's mind. Let him enjoy life when he could, when his Gift let him alone.

In the Waegmunding clan, many of the males had been born with magical skills. Aelfhere's grandson Wiglaf had the Gift of true seeing. Visions of true events came to him. They came when they would, whether Wiglaf was awake or asleep, and whether of past, present or future, the Gift never told. All too often the visions were terrible. Aelfhere pitied Wiglaf, but his own Gift, he thought, was harder to bear.

Aelfhere was able to read other people's minds. No, it was worse than that. He *had* to read them. Neverendingly the thoughts of others poured into his own mind: smallnesses, meannesses, desires, hatreds, sorrows. Over the years he had learned to make the mental voices of others quieter, but still he found it difficult to treat other people naturally. And they knew. Behind his back they made the sign against evil.

Ecgtheow, father of the mighty Beowulf, had been another Waegmunding whose Gift had hurt more than helped him. He had the Gift of self-righteous anger that always gave him strength when he thought he most needed it. But the Gift provided no judgment. In the end Ecgtheow killed a man, and so he had to flee his own country to the land of the Danes where King Hrothgar kindly took him in. Hrothgar also paid off the dead man's relatives, thus allowing Ecgtheow to leave. It was a mighty generosity King Hrothgar showed Ecgtheow, and always Ecgtheow meant to repay it. But he was afraid to mix in with people after that, afraid that his Gift would rise again and hurt him. And

so he wasted the rest of his days avoiding conflict, and the Danish king's generosity went unpaid.

Only Ecgtheow's son, Aelfhere's kinsman Beowulf, had a Gift that was seemingly easy to bear. He had been Gifted with the strength and endurance of thirty men, and that Gift had led him to a kingdom.

Aelfhere had once been very close to Beowulf. He only heard of him now. Beowulf, King of the Geats, must be an old man, but his kingdom was peaceful and he was deeply respected by his people. How different from the start of it all! Then Beowulf and he, two Waegmundings alone at the court of King Hygelac of the Geats, had needed all their pride in themselves and each other. The two of them were always outsiders in those days, always the ones people laughed at, even though they had been picked as fosterlings by the former king, Hygelac's father, and even though Beowulf was Hygelac's own nephew.

It was, as usual, the fault of the Waegmunding Gifts. As the two boys approached manhood and their Gifts began to exert themselves, they became clumsy in their new powers, hurting themselves and others. Aelfhere would stare at people in shocked dismay, overhearing their thoughts and even repeating them aloud, making enemies of almost everyone at King Hygelac's court. Beowulf boasted of his strength and then fell over his spear; he obeyed the arms master's orders exactly and somehow broke his wooden sword on the target every time; he interfered in arguments and finished by bloodying everyone's nose, including his own.

Beowulf's uncle, King Hygelac, often honored others — Breca, Heardred, Hereric — with gifts of armor and jeweled weapons. Never, though, did he honor Aelfhere or Beowulf. Aelfhere was training as a skald and would have preferred a gift of a harp or even a drum over armor and weapons. But Beowulf, who worshiped his uncle Hygelac and wanted only to be first warrior on Hygelac's mead bench, was deeply hurt. He never forgot those early injuries. All his life he did what he did because of them.

The embers glowed paler, and the little wolf cub began to snore. Aelfhere shook himself. The past was the past. It was time to sleep.

He stirred herbs into the cup of water one of the slaves had left warm by the fire. He sipped. Too many minds bombarding his own over the course of the day; too much to bear witness to. And so he needed herbs to help him sleep.

Beowulf had needed no herbs for *his* Gift.

"Neh, neh," the old man muttered aloud. It shamed him to think that way. Had he not kept vigil on the cold Baltic shore while Beowulf, scarcely older than Wiglaf was now, took on that swimming contest with Breca? Fully armored and carrying his sword, Beowulf had easily kept pace with Breca, but then they encountered sea serpents. Thinking to win his uncle Hygelac's favor, Beowulf fought the monsters while Breca swam the rest of the course and won. The entire court of King Hygelac had laughed at Beowulf when he came back, exhausted after seven days in the sea and proclaiming he had killed nine sea monsters. It didn't matter that Aelfhere bore witness to the truth of Beowulf's deeds. People thought it was only two Waegmundings siding together.

In the shadows beyond the fire Wiglaf moaned. Aelfhere looked carefully. The boy was awake. At least, his eyes were open. But his Gift had come to him. He was in his vision trance.

Aelfhere rubbed uselessly at his temples. His own Gift was stirring. Images from Wiglaf's vision painted themselves in Aelfhere's mind. He tried not to see what Wiglaf was seeing, but it was utterly impossible to blind himself or quieten the thoughts Wiglaf projected at him. A filthy hag crooning to herself in a wave-lapped cave lit by magical were-fire — now leaping to her feet to greet a monster splashing out of the sea that bordered the cave. This monster was more lizard than man, though he had arms and legs like a human. Both arms and legs were very long and muscular and ended in claws like steel spikes. Head and shoulders taller than the hag, the newcomer rumbled a laugh at her capering and dumped at her feet the contents of the bag he carried. This bag was made of glittering dragon scales and obviously magical, for a seemingly endless stream of human bodies spilled out of it, one, another, more — arms and legs entangled, loose heads rolling, here a hand, there an iron belt studded with garnets — and still the bodies came pouring out, greased with gore and sliding across their despoiled kin to make little red lakes of their own. Blood coursed in rivulets across the dank, bone-scattered floor. The hag crowed happily and bathed her hands in it.

Vile, vile. Aelfhere could see only through a wash of red. Half blind to the real world, he made himself walk to where Wiglaf sat rigid. The boy's face was sweaty with horror, and he had thrown off all his furs. Lhaerf, the wolf cub, quivered and whined under the bench.

"Neh, do not eat them, stop!" Wiglaf shouted to the images of his vision. He punched air wildly.

"Wiglaf, boy, let them go! Wake!"

The dream vanished. Aelfhere sighed deeply.

"Grandfather!" Wiglaf's eyes were white and round. "You saw? All those warriors dead? You saw? And the hag's nails — she dragged one of the bodies to her with a single finger —"

The boy was too old for it but Aelfhere knelt by the sleeping bench and held him tightly. "Hush, then, eh, hush," he murmured into Wiglaf's ear. "It happened years ago. There is nothing anyone can do now for those good men in Grendel's bag. Their gnawed bones are long dust."

"You know of that creature — Grendel?"

"Yes, I know Grendel. No one who has seen him could ever forget it. As for the hag — Grendel's mother she was, as evil as her son and twice as dangerous. I never saw her except through Beowulf's eyes, but they painted a good image." He halted. His face grew stern. "This is the fourth true vision you have had involving Beowulf, is it not?"

Wiglaf stiffened. "Not again, Grandfather! A few visions are no reason for me to leave you to serve Beowulf! I am happy here."

"Happiness doesn't mean rightness, boy. Our clan is dying —"

"Anyway, I don't see how this latest vision has anything to do with Beowulf."

Aelfhere looked at the boy's jutting chin and sighed. "You must know the story of Beowulf and Grendel. I've sung it often enough at banquets. Or were you always too busy eating to listen?"

Still shaking a little, Wiglaf reached for Lhaerf. With great concentration he worked his fingers into the downy fur behind the wolf pup's ears. Lhaerf slowly settled in his lap, sighing with contentment. At last Wiglaf said, "Grendel the troll. I remember some of the tale. There was a Danish king —"

"Hrothgar," Aelfhere said with a nod.

"— and he'd built a great mead hall. It had a name —"

"Heorot," Aelfhere said. "And I bear witness that there was never another mead hall greater. It was huge, much bigger even than Beowulf's. Its roof gleamed like a field of wheat blown by summer winds. A magnificent rack of stag antlers was mounted in the gable and the tines would catch the sun and shine as if gilded themselves. Even when I saw it, neglected and despoiled, it was plain that this was the greatest mead hall in all the world."

Wiglaf smiled. "Shall I fetch your harp, Grandfather?"

"So it is plain language you want?" Aelfhere said, mustering dignity. "Well, then, it was Grendel who despoiled Heorot. He hated humans, and King Hrothgar and his Danes lived near enough to him that he couldn't prevent himself hearing the sounds of their singing and laughter. So he went to Heorot one night when all the warriors were drunk or asleep and he killed and ate fifteen on the spot, and killed and took away fifteen others."

"The ones I dreamed?"

"Eh, gods help you."

Wiglaf was silent, dark and small and seeming now older than the boy he was. His fingers stopped scratching, and in his lap Lhaerf whined.

"Nor were the thirty dead men the end of it," Aelfhere went on. "Night after night Grendel came to Heorot, and night after night he killed and ate, killed and ate. Not a warrior among the Danes could touch him. People said he had a magic spell on him, that no weapon could hurt him or even pierce his skin. No one could find his lair. Eventually warriors stopped sleeping in Heorot. Then the evening banquets stopped. Soon Heorot was used only in daylight hours, and then only for Hrothgar and his counselors to puzzle over what to do about Grendel. Twelve years had passed and Grendel still owned the mead hall from dusk to dawn. The story was making fools of the Danes. When I first saw it, that glorious mead hall was cold and damp, with no more fire in its hearth than this little one here. Spiders had made webs of the rafters, and the walls were bare. The mead benches were all put away. The building stank of its shame."

"You and Beowulf went to King Hrothgar's court to stop Grendel, then?"

"Beowulf needed to prove himself, do you see?" Aelfhere said. "King Hygelac still laughed at him. *Come with me, Aelfhere*, Beowulf said to me. *I will kill that troll with my bare hands. And then, when it's over, you and others will say what you saw me do.*" Aelfhere grimaced.

"And did you see it?"

"I have sung it so, many a time."

"Tell it to me again."

"When you will listen, for once?"

Wiglaf grinned. "Did you always listen when you were my age and the old skalds sang?"

"Eh, then. Listen now!

"We were two at first, Waegmundings both. Beowulf needed more witnesses. Thirteen he sought, the keenest of warriors and stout wave-walkers to cross the whale-way to Hrothgar's realm two days to the south."

"Grandfather," Wiglaf said. "The story would go better with fewer wave-walkers and whale-ways."

Aelfhere hid a smile. "A warrior you will clearly be, Wiglaf. Agreed then. Less poetry, and less criticism both.

"What happened," he went on, "is that Beowulf asked King Hygelac's permission to take a ship and oarsmen and go to help King Hrothgar's Danes in their problem with Grendel. Hygelac was obviously sure we would all be killed, but he gave his permission anyway. We fifteen weren't worth much to him on the mead bench, I suppose.

"We made ready. We embarked. The ship was bright with our armor and weapons. The oarsmen hardly had time to tire before the wind took us up, embracing us like a bird with foamy breast — do not laugh, boy! — eh, well, like a boat with a decent sail and the wind in the right direction. By the second day we could see the headlands of the Danish realm shining off our bow. We dragged the boat up onto the beach and anchored it.

"Then a Dane on horseback rode up to us — a coast warden of courage he was — and after a little spear-waving, he asked us who we were and what we wanted in the land of the Danes. He addressed all his questions to Beowulf, though none of us were especially marked as leader. But then, of course, Beowulf had on his magical coat of mail, made by Wayland Smith in the days when gods roamed the earth. It made him stand out, big all over as he was. His boar-capped helmet, too; I remember the sun gleaming on the cheek-guards. And there was something about his eyes — eh, then, you said I was not to be poetic, so I'll just mention that the gray in them could go almost silver if he was angry, and the blue always reminded me of the winter sky. And his jaw would set in boar-determination when he *would* do a thing, no matter its danger..."

"He is very brave," Wiglaf said. "I saw as much in my other visions."

"Brave, eh, eh. Men are always brave when they have nothing to lose. Well, then, Beowulf told the coast warden the truth: that we served King Hygelac of the Geats, but that we had come to do King Hrothgar a service. And Beowulf mentioned that his father Ecgtheow was known to King Hrothgar. It was enough to get us up the cliffs and on the road to Heorot.

"The way was prosperous. *This at least Grendel has not despoiled*, I remember Handscio saying. The road was tiled right up to the wall surrounding the mead hall, and all along it were cattle, and horses roamed the pastures, and people worked the ripening fields of corn.

"We made our way to the wall through a crowd of Danish freemen. No one spoke to us and no one smiled. A herald accosted us at the gate, telling us to lay down our weapons and announce our business. Beowulf answered him graciously, naming himself and asking leave to speak to King Hrothgar in person. We sat then, our spears and shields leaning against the wall, waiting for the herald to return.

"He was smiling when he came back, and invited us in. We left Eamund and Handscio to guard our weapons and followed the herald. *Is it true that you have the strength of thirty men in your grip?* the herald asked Beowulf.

"*You will see*, Beowulf answered him shortly.

"*I am told you once lived here.*

"*I was only a baby*, Beowulf replied. *But I have a blood debt to repay in thanks to your King Hrothgar.*

"That was his father Ecgtheow's debt, of course," Aelfhere told Wiglaf. "But it was not just to repay his father's debt to the Danes that Beowulf wanted to kill Grendel. He wanted to prove himself to Hygelac. Also, of course, it would gain the Danes as allies for the Geats, no small thing in war-beset times."

"Do you think he wanted to be king after Hygelac, even then?" Wiglaf asked.

"Neh, boy. He only wanted to please his uncle." Aelfhere tugged an end of the fur blanket over the boy's knees. "Are you sure you are not sleepy yet?"

"In the middle of a story?"

"Eh, well, then we were all inside Heorot. It was a shock. First, it stank — like horse piss, only worse. The walls were bare of hangings and marked with ugly symbols, the roof pillars likewise. The gable windows

were blocked with birds' nests, the fire barely flickering, and Hrothgar was an old man on his golden throne at the far end of the hall, his long gray hair braided under its circlet of thin gold. A sorry sight, gray hair on gray beard, shoulders hunched as if to protect himself from bad news, but smiling, smiling, holding out his arms to greet Beowulf. *Then are you Beowulf, that babe of old I kept safe when even your father could not do so?* Ah, how quickly did he stamp his claim! But the skald at his feet on the dais looked upon us as if we were something moldy hanging in a market stall. That was Unferth. He didn't want anyone but himself to help or advise his king.

"Beowulf made a long and gracious speech honoring King Hrothgar and our King Hygelac. He then proclaimed his own mighty deeds, which were not many — he had to include the battle with the sea monsters — and he asked Hrothgar's permission to let us stay overnight in the hall to fight Grendel. In return he asked only, if Fate willed his death, that someone might take his special armor back to Hygelac.

"Hrothgar warned of the many who had already died, but when Beowulf was unswayed, the Danish king accepted his offer and immediately willed it that Heorot be prepared for a banquet."

"Stink and all?" Wiglaf asked.

"They did what they could. Fresh dirt for the floor, rushes everywhere, the swallows' nests swept away, doors opened wide — and then there were the good smells of cooking. The tapestries were rehung, the mead benches set up, and the fire burned high. It was well enough when we sat down to eat."

Wiglaf said teasingly, "Especially when the mead cup made its rounds?"

"We drank, as who wouldn't? Some drank more than they should. Hrothgar's skald, Unferth, was one. When he'd drunk himself brave, he jeered at Beowulf about that ridiculous swimming contest with Breca. But Beowulf mastered Unferth, first by telling the truth about what happened in the contest and then by pointing out that Breca, and indeed Unferth, had never bloodied a sword in battle, especially against Grendel. It was well done," Aelfhere finished. "The mead hall was for Beowulf from that time forward."

"And did you then sing, Grandfather?"

"I did. And Unferth, too, to give him credit. *And* people listened, and cheered when we were finished. Then Hrothgar's beauteous queen brought round the beaker of mead, and when she got to Beowulf he pledged to kill Grendel for her or be himself killed. After that, I had quiet words with Unferth. He was a reliable teller of tales, though a troublemaker. There was, he said, a tale of Heorot hill being an ancient burial place. Unferth had sung the tale to King Hrothgar, but that had not prevented Hrothgar building Heorot right on the mound's summit."

"Who did the tale say was buried there?"

"Giants, Unferth told me. Buried by giant-kin who had the power to cast spells."

Aelfhere was silent for a moment. Wiglaf said, "Grendel was a troll, though, not a giant. Could *he* have used spells — ?"

"I know only what happened that night. The banquet ended before darkness fell. No Dane wanted to be there when Grendel came. They took down the tapestries before leaving, to save them from anticipated blood." Aelfhere laughed ironically. "But at least they left us sleeping benches."

"But who among you would sleep, with Grendel coming?"

"All of us, it turned out, save myself and Beowulf. I had to pace to keep my own eyes from closing, and all the while carrying Beowulf's war corselet, his helmet and his sword, for he was firm that he would fight Grendel hand to hand or not at all. He had told the others that they should not attack Grendel with weapons; that they were to watch only, unless clearly needed. He rested then on his sleeping bench but remained watchful, leaning on one elbow. The other men slept at once, as if safe in the shelter of Hygelac's mead hall instead of in Heorot, awaiting a fiend. It was unnatural, that. I had good cause then to remember Unferth's tale of spell-casting.

"And all the time Grendel was coming. I picture him now, that walker in shadow, parting the moor mists on his winding path to Heorot. I imagine him grinning with glee to see the smoke from the roof hole, knowing that for the first time in years the hall was night-occupied. The bolts were locked, but what was that to a troll? He smashed them open with a single blow. I stood in the shadows near the far wall as the door swung inward on broken hinges. And as Grendel entered our hall and gazed around it with balefire in his eyes, no matter how I tried, I could not move.

"Beowulf, too, was still. Later he blamed himself for what happened then, but I do not think there was anything he could have done. Until

Grendel had actually spilled blood — had fed the earth of the tomb on which Heorot sat — I believe the mead hall was Grendel's to do with as he liked. And so it was that, unopposed, the evil one seized on the nearest of the Geats — Handscio, it was, the youngest of us all — and killed him.

"Grendel thought then to reach for another of us, but this time, the first ever, there was a hand eagerly seeking his own. While the rest of the sleepy Geats staggered to their feet, Beowulf had already leaped the central hearth fire, and there he was squeezing the monster's hand in his grip of thirty men. In the raging hunger of Grendel's thoughts I recognized sudden astonishment and fear. Grendel had never been afraid before, never known what it was to imagine failure. He howled like a chained wolf.

"From one side of the hall to the other the hand-linked pair lurched and stumbled, scattering coals from the fire, shattering benches, battering at each other with their free hands, and all the while Grendel howled and Beowulf maintained his grim silence. The Geats forgot what Beowulf had ordered and, weapons drawn, encircled the fighting pair. *Out of the way!* Beowulf shouted, as spears and swords came at them.

"This was where I could help. I dropped Beowulf's battle gear and joined the fray, pulling away first one comrade, then another. I shouted to the others, *The fiend cannot be harmed with weapons! It is Beowulf you endanger, not Grendel!* Finally the men saw sense and withdrew to the far corners of the hall.

"Now, still crushing the monster's hand, Beowulf pushed Grendel up against King Hrothgar's throne. Then with both hands Beowulf lifted and twisted the arm attached to the fiend's ruined hand. Grendel screamed. Higher and higher that arm went, the angle horrible to see, Beowulf sweating and groaning with effort, higher and higher — it could go no farther, but it did. With a terrible ripping sound the shoulder tore asunder. *This is for Handscio!* Beowulf shouted, as Grendel, shrieking in agony, twisted himself free and headed for the door, leaving his arm in Beowulf's grasp.

"Panting, Beowulf sank to the floor. I found an unbroken beaker with some ale still in it and passed it to him. He dropped the troll's monstrous arm in the dirt and drank thirstily, leaning against the throne. The others gathered round, murmuring with awe. *No one, not even Grendel, could survive the blood loss from this*, someone said.

"Meanwhile some of the Danes arrived. They began to pass Grendel's arm from one person to the next, some staggering under its surprising weight, others staring in horror at the steel spikes that had served Grendel for fingernails. *It is an honor of war*, someone said, and at that three of the Danes took the arm and fastened it to the gabled roof. Someone else rebuilt the fire, so that the arm could be clearly seen.

"Then Hrothgar came, and Unferth the skald, and Hrothgar's queen, and amid all the cheering and laughter those three approached Beowulf, who scrambled to his feet. *You have rescued my hall, Beowulf*, Hrothgar said. *You have assuaged our long shame and our grief. Skalds the world over will sing of your deeds. Henceforward I shall love you and honor you as my own son.*

"The old king stood up straight, and I hadn't realized until then how tall he was. He hugged Beowulf to him for a brief moment, and then the queen kissed him on both cheeks. The king's voice echoed through the suddenly quiet hall. *Heorot shall be cleansed of all trace of Grendel's evil-doings*, he proclaimed. *By tomorrow's sunset nowhere in the world will there be a hall more beautiful. And then we shall have a banquet such as Heorot has never seen. Honors shall be given to Beowulf, whose fame for killing Grendel will endure through all the ages.*

"*It was done most willingly*, Beowulf replied. *I only wish I could have seen the troll breathe his last. At dawn I will follow his trail to be sure of his death.*

"Few then returned to bed, but Beowulf did, sleeping sound and deep. I wakened him when the sun rose. Many Danes and Geats joined us in following the staggering footsteps and blood trail of a monster heading to its final home. Merry we all were, cheering and laughing, and Unferth made up a song of Beowulf's deeds as we went."

"Did he include the race with Breca?" Wiglaf asked.

"Yes, and the sea monsters had increased to a dozen. I laughed inside myself, but Beowulf didn't seem to mind. He had waited many years for the first skald to sing of him.

"Finally, the moorland trail began to descend, and as we followed it through the thorny tangle of brush and misshapen trees, we came to a gorge dug by a stream looking for the sea. It was an evil place, where rocks tumbled over gravel and wild grasses caught the unwary foot, but the gouts of blood showed that Grendel had taken that path. We did as well. Eventually we came to a place where we could see a cove beneath us. The water rolled dizzyingly and seemed almost to bubble, the result of the pounding waves of the open ocean that could not enter the narrow fiord between the two steep headlands on either side of us. And here, even though it must have been some hours since Grendel arrived, the waters welled thickly red.

"*So much blood! He is surely dead,* Hrothgar declared, and not one of us thought any different.

"*Did he throw himself into the mere to drown?* someone asked.

"*There are many sea caves in this coast,* Unferth replied. *Some never show their undersea mouths, but thrust themselves upward under the land we call our own. Perhaps one of these was Grendel's goal.*

"*Wounded animals always seek their lairs to die,* Beowulf said.

"Everyone but Beowulf was happy. Only he wished for final proof of Grendel's death. And who can blame him? He had seen too well the need for proofs of wondrous deeds.

"If there had been a banquet in Heorot the night before, Wiglaf, you should have just seen the one we had that night! The food came endlessly, course after course, duck and swan and roasted larks, all served on platters of silver and gold. And the gifts! Ah, Hrothgar proved himself a great king in his gift-giving that night. Horses, armor, weapons .... And the queen gave gifts as well, golden rings and the most gorgeous collar since the gods fought over the Brising's necklace. Between courses we sat over our ale and our mead, and always there was someone singing or harping, always a tale to be told. Dragon-slayers we heard of, and a Frisian massacre of hall-guests, and a king who had grown up with every possible advantage but ended in banishment after the worst of all rules. And ever the skalds compared old heroes to Beowulf, who they said was like to be one of the greatest rulers of men ever.

"At this Beowulf protested that his uncle Hygelac was King of the Geats and that Hygelac's son would follow him to the throne. *And that will suit me very well,* he finished."

"And was Grendel really dead?" Wiglaf asked. "And what of the hag, his mother?"

"You are too impatient, boy. A story can be told properly, or it can be rounded to four words: *And thus it finished.* Which is it to be this time?"

"Properly, please," the boy said meekly.

"Eh, then. And so in time the banquet came to an end, and eventually the drinking, too, and Beowulf was put in another chamber for the rest of the night — a place of honor for a hero. The rest of us, and a lot

of the Danes, made ready to sleep in Heorot, for no one now feared that Grendel would come again. And he did not, because he was indeed dead. But someone else did."

"The hag!" Wiglaf burst out before he could stop himself.

"I saw it happen," Aelfhere said. "I never sleep well, and that night I was possessed of a feeling of foreboding. I was hardly surprised when Grendel's mother burst in through the unlocked doors. But when I tried to move or shout I could not. She freed her son's arm from the gable, then used her foul nails to slit the throat of one of the Danes as he lay sleeping. Instantly she grappled him in her merciless grip, and was gone at once with his body. I have never seen woman so strong or swift."

"It was to avenge Grendel?" Wiglaf asked. "A death for his death?"

"One cannot claim the honor avenging of a fiend like Grendel. That monster had killed hundreds of warriors over the years by spells and other dishonest means. His death was fair punishment for crimes and was therefore by law not to be avenged. But his mother was evil, Wiglaf, very evil. And the victim she chose that night was Hrothgar's favorite counselor. Hrothgar wept long when I told him.

"*Bring Beowulf to him*, ordered the queen.

"I went to Beowulf's chamber and told him what had happened. Then we went together to where Hrothgar sat, head bowed and shoulders shaking. *What ails the king that he must weep so?* Beowulf demanded.

"At that Hrothgar raised his head. *Dead is Eshere, my sage adviser, comrade at arms and dearest friend. Grendel's mother has killed and taken him away.*

"*Better to let me avenge your friend than mourn him*, Beowulf said. *I promise you, I will kill this troll woman for you, or myself die trying.*

"The old king leaped up. *You will do this? Great will I reward you, warrior-son.* He paused. *But I would not have you die when I have only just found you.*

"*Each of us must die*, Beowulf said, *and glory before death is a warrior's worthiest fate. I ask only that, if I do die, all that you have given me will be sent to my uncle, King Hygelac, that he might know how you esteem me.*"

Aelfhere shook his head sadly. "Do you see it, Wiglaf? Those years he sat without honor on his uncle's mead bench had marked him truly. The ill-deeds visited upon a child never quite go away.

"Eh, eh. Well, King Hrothgar pledged he would do as Beowulf asked. Then he promised warriors to attend to Beowulf's every command.

"*I would have those whose words are never doubted*, Beowulf said.

"I knew what that meant. He was going to go after the troll-hag by himself and wanted witnesses to his courage. *There is no need for you to do this on your own, Beowulf,* I said. But he would not listen. And in the end he was right, because none among us could have survived what awaited Beowulf that day.

"The journey to the cove was a silent one. Yesterday we had laughed to see the gouts of blood, but today the blood trail was Eshere's. When we got to the gorge we saw a terrible thing. Eshere's head had been torn from his body and stuck upon a stake facing uphill, as if in mocking greeting. Hrothgar's jaw set, and he ordered that the head be taken back to Heorot. One by one, then, we passed that stake down the gorge to the rocks overlooking the cove. It was before noon, but as we descended, it seemed that darkness was gathering. The open sea spurted against the headlands, and the water of the cove, reddened with what was left of Eshere's blood, moaned in reply.

"*I hunted a stag here once, long ago,* one of the Danes announced in the silence that had fallen over us all. *I and my hounds chased the stag to the very edge of this cove. You would have thought it would leap into the cove to swim for freedom, but it did not. Instead, it looked shuddering at the water, then turned to face my hounds leaping for its throat. It died rather than go into that water.*

"*I would die rather than not go in,* Beowulf said. *Grendel's lair, and his mother's, is down there somewhere, and I will find it before you will see me again.* He turned to King Hrothgar, sitting anxious on the rock beside him. *Please remember what I asked of you. I would that Hygelac my king will know, by the treasures you have given me, that I have achieved your esteem.*

"*You have achieved it greatly,* King Hrothgar replied. *I will keep my pledge to you. Your treasures shall be his if you do not return to us, though I hope and trust that you will.*

"By this time there were many worm-like things looping the reddened water of the cove, and other beasts on the rocks nearby," Aelfhere told Wiglaf. "It seemed they understood what Beowulf meant to do, for they let forth a tremendous din. Our battle horns were scarcely enough to be heard over their noise. One monster, tusked and hideous, we brought down with a spear, and the others slipped away into the water until it near boiled with all their commotion. Seeing this, Beowulf stood thoughtful, and then he said, *I will wear my mail and helmet and sword, for the monsters here will do the hag's will, if they can.*

"*But the weight,* Unferth protested. *It will drag you down!*

"*I have done this before,* Beowulf reminded him. *Breca won a swimming contest because my sword was busy killing sea serpents. I wore armor then, too, and it did not stop me either killing the monsters or swimming home.*

"*Your strength now is greater even than then,* I told him. *But your sword is old. Beware of striking too powerfully, or it might break.*

"*You may take my sword,* Unferth offered suddenly. *Its name is Hrunting, and of heirlooms here it is easily the best. Its blade was etched with poison, and it has been battle-hardened by the blood of many ancient foes. Never has it been defeated.*

"*I thank you,* Beowulf replied, taking it, and without further word he leaped into the water. And so it was that Unferth's sword went where Unferth himself dared not go."

"He jumped into that water all full of monsters and blood?" Wiglaf asked, shuddering so that the little wolf cub scrambled from his lap, disappearing into shadows. "I couldn't have done that."

Aelfhere nodded. "Nor I. But in a way I did go with him, for as I sat on the rock my Gift came to life, and I saw what Beowulf had to endure in the underwater hell he had now entered. Sea serpents and nicors attacked him from every side, yet he was not afraid. He killed them all without taking a single injury himself. I lost track of time except to note that the sun had come to noon and passed it and still he fought in that underwater murk of monsters. His lungs were like no man's in the world, but even he was feeling the agonizing need to breathe when all at once the monsters drew back. He looked around wildly, but it was too late. The hag — a troll-woman with hair like weeds — had swum up behind him, then encircled him completely with her arms. Eh, Wiglaf, she was that much bigger than he! Her terrible nails dug for his skin, but his heirloom armor protected him. But he was almost dead now from lack of air to breathe. She realized this and dragged him off through the cold depths. Before very long she was splashing out beyond the tide line into a huge underwater cave, dragging Beowulf nearly unconscious behind her.

"He breathed then, great panting breaths of air that filled his mouth with the metallic taste of blood and his nose with the stench of foul droppings and rotting meat. Shadows flitted through the cave like creatures of darkness. Beowulf saw a firepit, but the flames in it seemed small for the eerie balefire that lit the cave. He saw sand and bones and piles of gold and scraps of flesh, and under a jutting cliff wall hung with scraps of cloth and other trophies he saw a huge pile of decaying dead men.

"The she-wolf let him drop but already those amazing lungs of his had revived him. He was on his feet before she could free her sharp, curved, dagger-like saex from its scabbard. Quickly, he raised Hrunting. The sword sang as it cut the air, but when it reached her unprotected skin it shuddered to a clanging stop. *So you, too, cannot be hit by normal weapons,* Beowulf got out through clenched teeth. He threw Hrunting to the ground. *Well, my grip alone was enough for Grendel. So shall it be for you.*

"*You're the one who killed my son,* she howled, and was after him like three boars at once. He fell under the furious onslaught, and she flung herself upon him. Half stunned, he was for a moment unable to move, weary from his battles with the sea monsters and nauseated by the terrible sights and smells of the cave. The she-troll sensed victory. Straddling his chest, holding him down with all the strength of her powerful legs, she brought the gleaming blade of her saex swift as Fate toward his neck.

"But Beowulf was quicker. Somehow he got hold of her wrists. The curved blade moved up and back. Then, with his hands still gripping her wrists, he squeezed with all his might, hoping that she would be like Grendel, whose bones were his as soon as he brought his strength to bear on them. But the hag was stronger than her son, or perhaps it was only that Beowulf was weary from all his battling and sickened by the smell of her breath. The most he could do was to keep her saex away from him. Even at that she did not give up, clenching his ribs with her bony knees, snarling and coming for his neck with her fangs.

"For the first time in his life Beowulf knew that he was overmatched. This time, without Fate's help, his Waegmunding Gift would not save him. In desperation he brought his knees up to slam against what he hoped would be the she-troll's kidneys. Then as he felt her take the blow, he shoved her backwards and down, rolling to one side before letting go of her wrists and leaping up. Like a snake she twisted the other way, but not before Beowulf saw, hanging on the trophy wall, a gigantic sword gleaming with its own were-fire. He had not seen it before, but Fate showed it to him now, a magical blade certainly — plunder from the giants' tomb under Heorot, perhaps. It was certainly the biggest, sharpest blade he had ever seen. Beowulf leaped for the sword while the hag scrambled to her feet and came after him with her saex. Now he had the giant's sword, monstrously heavy. Somehow he was on top of a rock nearly halfway across the cave; somehow the she-troll was beside him, her neck within sword-reach. *Fate be with me*, he muttered, and swung the sword.

"She died on her feet, her head cut right off. As Beowulf jerked the blade free it blazed joyously, brightening the whole cave until it seemed noon had come to this underground place. Into that vast brightness the she-troll toppled. Dark and thick her blood streamed across the sea strand and into the water that bounded her cave. Endless it seemed, a river of blood feeding a hungry sea, and for a short while Beowulf could only stand and watch in awe, with the giant's magic sword still held aloft. The sea water thickened and clotted, so crimson that Beowulf knew the watchers on the rocks beside the cove would be certain to see it."

"Well, did they?" Wiglaf prompted, when his grandfather stopped.

Aelfhere shook himself. "In fact they did, but I was too much in the thrall of my Gift to know that Hrothgar and his Danes decided that the blood staining the cove must be Beowulf's. He had been gone so long, you see, that they had been thinking he must surely be drowned. They were already mourning when the waters of the cove became stained with murky blood, and they assumed his drowned body had become the plaything for monsters. The Danes left, sagging with their grief, but we Geats remained. Eamund told me later that it was my own trance that kept our little force keeping vigil by the cove, though not one of the watchers believed that Beowulf was still living — except me, and I could not say so.

"A man who has almost died rejoices when the enemy takes his place, and so Beowulf did then. With a triumphant shout he made two-handed circles in the air with the gigantic sword that had saved his life. Then he began thinking again. *Eh, then, this is one weapon that can do injury to the troll-kind. If only Grendel's body is near. A head is better proof of death than an arm that has been torn off and later stolen ...*

"Beowulf leaped down from the rock and headed for the far reaches of the cave. There were piles of gems and gold amid the waste of the dead, but he didn't stop for them. For there in an adjoining cave lay Grendel, gape-mouthed in the dazzling sword-light, with the agony still staring from his dead eyes. *To avenge all you have killed!* Beowulf shouted,

bringing the giant sword whistling down, severing the dead troll's head so thoroughly that the body it had been attached to actually sprang into the air.

"The sword-light dimmed all at once. Beowulf examined the weapon. The blade was quietly melting into icicles. Scarcely able to believe his eyes, Beowulf plunged the sword into the sand to cleanse it of blood, but it made no difference. The blade-fire died altogether, and the blade continued to melt. At last there was nothing left of the giant's sword but the jeweled hilt in Beowulf's hand.

"*A true gift of Fate*, Beowulf said resignedly. He shoved the hilt into his belt and picked up Grendel's head, staggering under the weight. Then he went back to the main cave to take the hag's head likewise. He strained and strained, but his great strength had been temporarily used up. He knew he couldn't manage the weight of the hag's head as well as Grendel's. There was nothing for it but to take only one of the two. He chose Grendel's, as having done the most harm to Hrothgar, and left the she-troll there, her death unproven.

"Sadly Beowulf picked up Unferth's sword Hrunting. He had come to this terrible place to kill the hag, and had done so. But would it be as before, when the world refused to believe in his great deed because no one had witnessed it?"

"Couldn't he have gone back to the trolls' lair later and carried her up?" Wiglaf asked.

"He could have," responded Aelfhere, "but this time there was no one who refused to believe his tale. He rose to the surface through the roiling waters and hailed us. My comrades were so astonished and happy that more than a few of them wept. *You are alive!* they cried.

"*Of course I am alive*, said he. *Did you not wait for me here because you knew that I would return? Come, then, help me with this thing.* And he rolled Grendel's head across the rocky shore toward us. Even I, who had seen the whole set of events in my mind's eye, was silenced by the open-mouthed agony of that monstrous head. It took four men to lift it, while Beowulf came dripping from the sea.

"We wasted little time. Talk could wait until Hrothgar's court knew Beowulf was alive after all. We were fourteen Geats and one troll's head come to call at the king's mead hall. Ah, the shouts and the singing as we approached Heorot, the claps on the back! Beowulf was alive! The troll-woman and her son were dead! And four of the Danes took

Grendel's hideous head from us and carried it aloft into the hall, while Beowulf followed, mounted victoriously on the shoulders of others.

"Great was the rejoicing! And while fresh beakers of ale were passed to the newcomers, Beowulf told his tale. I bear witness that he did not embellish it. He told the raw truth about his own weakness, his need for Fate's help, and his inability to bring both bodies with him. But there was no dishonor given him for it, only the more love for his modest honesty.

"He ended at last. Then, almost as an afterthought, he presented to King Hrothgar the hilt of the Fate-given sword, dazzling with gems and covered with runes that told the story of the ending of the race of giants.

"*So also end the troll-kind, Fate willing,* Hrothgar said, then raised the hilt aloft so all could see it. *This I say true, no better hero ever lived than Beowulf, and no king is luckier than Hygelac, to have Beowulf as his thane.*

"Then there was Unferth, muttering lyrics to himself for the music he would sing in Beowulf's honor at the banquet that night. Beowulf returned to him his sword Hrunting, saying only soft words about it, even though it had proved useless against the trolls. And the banquet came and went as swiftly as the lark flies before the sun. Bittersweet was this feast, for we knew it would be the last. We had done what we came to do, and it was time to go home.

"Very early the next morning we fourteen met Hrothgar in farewell. To the king Beowulf pledged willingness to return at any time he might be needed, and suggested an alliance between the Geats and the Danes forever. Weeping a little at the departure of one he had come to love as a son, Hrothgar declared for all to hear, *As long as I rule this realm let the hoards and needs of Dane and Geat be common. And should it come to pass that Hygelac's son and heir die untimely, I deem it wise that you, Beowulf, be chosen king over all the Geats. In this I have no power, but I foresee many greatnesses for you, oh, my hearth guest and adopted son.*

"Then into the hall they brought Beowulf twelve new treasures, in addition to the ones they had already given after Grendel's death. We were so laden that we had to use the horses given to Beowulf to bear some of the weight. Embracing the king and queen, Beowulf thanked them, and then, with joy in our hearts, we took the tiled road back to the shore. There we met the same trusty coast warden who had guarded our ship for us. To him Beowulf gave an heirloom sword mounted with gold, and this worthy warrior sat the higher on Hrothgar's mead bench ever afterward because of it.

"Into our ship's hold went a golden banner, a great and ancient sword, a silver coat of mail, all of which had belonged to an early king of the Danes; and there was Hrothgar's own silver saddle as well as the queen's bracelets of twisted gold, the mantle she herself had woven, many broad gold rings, and the wondrous necklace with its priceless gem, in addition to all the gold and silver beakers and adornments that had been given us only that morning. Oh, yes, and the eight horses had to be housed there, too. There was barely room in the ship for the fourteen of us! But no harm came from it. The wind was fair and we crossed the deeps to our own Geat headlands at a fine speed.

"High on the strand we hauled our ship, helped by King Hygelac's harbor guard and other lookers-on, and then we unloaded all the treasure. Eh, Wiglaf, eyes opened wide at us then! Up to Hygelac's haughty hall we marched. Beowulf walked erect and proud, but I knew that in his heart he was anxious about meeting his uncle the king. *It will fare well,* I told him. *The king will know you now for what you are.* And so indeed it proved. Hygelac was waiting on his throne when we arrived, and space had been cleared for us on the most honored mead bench."

"News of the treasure went before you, did it?" Wiglaf asked.

"Eh, boy, I can't deny that you are right. I never much liked Hygelac, as you have fathomed. He had let us go to what he was sure would be our deaths with scarce a word, but when we returned it was all heartiness and words of love. *What happened with your quest, kinsman Beowulf? Long I begged thee not to seek that slaughtering monster Grendel. My sad heart seethed to see you go. Fate be thanked that you are home safe again.*"

"What a liar, to say he'd begged you not to go!" Wiglaf exclaimed.

"What a king claims he said cannot easily be disputed. And Beowulf devoured Hygelac's words of concern and caring as a man does who has not eaten in many days."

Wiglaf crossed his arms over his chest. "I think I hate this Hygelac."

"You waste your energy. It all happened many years ago, and Hygelac is long dead. And Beowulf was happy. At banquet that night he sat in the first place on the most honored mead bench and gave to his beloved uncle or to his uncle's wife every single one of the treasures that King Hrothgar had given him, all except one horse and its silver saddle. In return, Beowulf received from Hygelac his grandfather's mighty heirloom sword and a huge tract of land. No one, even I, thought the return an unequal one. From that day Beowulf was his uncle's favorite of hall thanes.

"The years went by quickly, as years do when events are full of battle horns and bloodied swords. King Hygelac died in a raid on the Frisians; a few years later his son Heardred fell in battle with the Swedes. With Heardred's death all of Hygelac's direct male line had died out, and so it was that Beowulf was made king. I, as usual, made the song for it."

"Why did you leave Beowulf's hall, Grandfather?" Wiglaf asked.

"Under Beowulf's reign the land of the Geats was at peace from one border to the other. No one invaded Geatland, and Beowulf himself attacked no one he could not conquer. I sang his praises until there was nothing new to sing. My clan needed me more than he did. And so I left Beowulf and came here, married your grandmother who brought your father into the world. Then we waited forever until you came along. That is all you need to know. Now go to sleep."

Wiglaf yawned. "Beowulf was sad when you left?"

"He was sad. I was sad. Sleep!"

The boy screwed his eyes up tight and said no more. When his breathing was deep and even, Aelfhere went back to the fire. Moodily he poked a long stick at the glowing coals that were all that remained of the Waegmunding hearth fire.

Rumor had it that despite his age, Beowulf still practiced in the arms hall and rode every day. Certainly his court thrived. There were arms masters there, smiths, falconers, a wondrous stable of great horses, a mead hall full of hearth companions.

Wiglaf refused to be sent away from his grandfather, but a visit with Aelfhere to his famous kinsman would not seem threatening. Wiglaf could begin warrior training while his grandfather remained to see him safe and happy. This Waegmunding steading needed nothing from Aelfhere any more.

He nodded to himself. Yes, he would take Wiglaf to Beowulf's mead hall. He wrapped his cloak around himself and waited for dawn.

———

Wiglaf watched his grandfather, red-faced and grunting, tie the mysterious bundle onto the packhorse's back. It was a large, oddly shaped thing and obviously very heavy. Seven days on the road and Wiglaf had never once been allowed to touch it.

First thing this morning Grandfather had demanded to see the boy's cloak. He found all the trouble spots — the grease stain on the front, the place where the hem had started to unravel, the little hole where Wiglaf had snagged it on a branch. "A fine way to enter the court of a king, boy. I suppose your tunic is no better?"

It wasn't. "To the lake with you," Grandfather had ordered. "Wash the cloak, the tunic, those trousers and yourself, while you're at it! Hair, too. Braid it back the warrior's way. You look like an urchin!"

And so it was that while his grandfather packed the mysterious bundle onto the horse's back, Wiglaf, lighter-skinned than before and steaming in the morning sun, sat sharpening his knife. Wiglaf's father had given the knife to him after his mother's death, when he was but ten winters old. *We begin small. Gradually I will teach you larger weapons.* But there had been no other weapons. The plague that had killed his mother swept his father away as well. It had been Aelfhere who taught Wiglaf the throwing knife — *You think a skald cannot catch his own supper?* After four years Wiglaf's aim was nearly always true. He had killed Lhaerf's wolf mother with the knife, thinking of her as food instead of a nursing female. There had been three pups, but two had died. He had never used the knife on living quarry since.

At last Aelfhere was satisfied that the bundle was safely stowed. Wiglaf sheathed his knife and handed over the bedrolls, the food, Aelfhere's harp.

"We get there today?" he asked.

"Yes."

"One word?" Wiglaf grinned. "You take an entire song to describe the color of grass, Grandfather."

The day passed slowly, with their trail edging desolate bogs and crossing high, hilly moorlands without a single dwelling. But by mid-afternoon the land grew gentler. Away to their left Wiglaf could see the outline of high sea cliffs. "Eh, Geatland, at last," Aelfhere said. "Those headlands are the sign. Do you see the highest cliff, in the middle there?" Wiglaf nodded. "That is Hronesness — Cape of the Whales. Beneath it are the most dangerous shoals on all our coast."

Inland from the headlands stood cultivated fields with many out-buildings and houses much like those of the Waegmundings. The dirt trail became a proper road of trampled earth flagged with stone, and as they trudged along it the steadings became more numerous, each with their fields of oats and rye lining the road and their paddocks alive with the season's new colts and lambs. Now there were people working in the fields or coming out of their houses to stare at them. They were a tall and fair folk and well dressed, with mantles of many colors all fringed with red.

"Your harp says you are a skald," one old farmer called out to Aelfhere. "Are you to play for the king?"

"If he asks," Aelfhere answered shortly.

All looked curiously at the short, erect old man with traces of black still in his hair and beard, and the boy, small and dark, leading their packhorse. Wiglaf had never seen so many people all together in his life. He was relieved to reach the wall surrounding the royal village.

They were greeted by two guards at the gate. "Your names, sirs?" one said. They held long spears crossed and both had swords at their belts.

"Aelfhere, clan elder of the Waegmundings, and kinsman and former hearth companion of King Beowulf. This is my grandson, Wiglaf, also kinsman of the king."

At once one of the guards invited them to sit on a nearby bench and called for refreshments; the other sent a messenger to announce their presence to the king. Ale arrived only moments before the messenger came back, and to Wiglaf's astonished delight the king was with the messenger.

Beowulf was thinner and grayer and more lined than Wiglaf had seen him in his dreams but still quite muscular and erect. His hair was pulled back into careless warrior braids. He wore a spectacularly jeweled neck collar of layered gold, but otherwise his garments were just like his people's. Wiglaf smiled to himself at the fresh grease stain the king had somehow got on the tunic under the green overmantle. He liked Beowulf already.

Uncertainly, Wiglaf got to his feet and bowed. But the old king didn't see him.

"They were not lying!" he said to Aelfhere in a barrel-chested voice. "You really are here!" He pulled Aelfhere to his feet. "I don't believe it! Unchanged, I swear — except for turning badger at the beard." And King Beowulf laughed, a deep, rumbling joyousness, and engulfed Grandfather Aelfhere in a bear hug.

"You still have your strength of thirty men, I see," Aelfhere said when Beowulf gave him a chance to speak. He was trying to sound

dignified, but Wiglaf knew how pleased he was.

"Thirty *old* men, unfortunately. Ah, well, it serves. And did you really marry that lovely Breawu of yours? Clan elder you are now, they said. Ah, the songs you will have for me!"

"Eh, songs aplenty — and not all happy ones. Here is one, though, that is. Meet my grandson, your kinsman, Wiglaf son of Weohstan."

Now when Wiglaf bowed, the gray-blue eyes were on him. "A man already, I see, Aelfhere. Can the years really have been so many? But you carry only a knife, son of Weohstan. Are you then skald as well, like your grandfather?"

"Warrior, please, sir," Wiglaf got out. "And my knife is not *only* a knife. It was my father's and an heirloom before that. I pledge it against any arrow your men can shoot. Over short distances, anyway," he added honestly.

Again Beowulf laughed. "Warrior, then. I shall have a place made for you on my highest mead bench."

"Thank you, sir," Wiglaf said, bowing low and flushing. "But such is too much honor for me. I have no other war gear, and could not use it if I did."

"Honest, I see," Beowulf said approvingly. "The place is yours, regardless. We shall find for you a sword and spear, a corselet of mail and a helmet. My arms master will soon make sure you can use them."

Aelfhere was smiling. "It was for this moment that I have broken my back seven times in the last week." He turned to the messenger. "Could you fetch for me the bundle tied to my packhorse outside?"

In a moment the man was back with the oddly shaped bundle Wiglaf had wondered about all week. Aelfhere took it, then said to his grandson, "These were your father's, Wiglaf. They were once owned by Swedish kings, and are of mighty lineage. Your father won them honorably on the field of battle. Unwrap your battle gear, Wiglaf son of Weohstan."

There was a shield, linden yellow encircled and bossed with bronze; a gold-bright helmet; a coat of ringed mail with breastplates of bronze gilt with silver; and, in a sheath of smoothly polished wood and ivory, an ancient sword of priceless beauty, its two edges so fine and sharp they could have been hammered by dwarfs in times of old. One item after another, Aelfhere gave them to Wiglaf, helping him put on the helmet and coat of mail. It was all too big, but Wiglaf ran his hands over

it lovingly. When he had blinked enough times to see clearly, he looked up at his grandfather, but Aelfhere and Beowulf were chatting together companionably, and neither of them seemed to have the slightest interest in Wiglaf.

He swung the sword tentatively, then again. "Not like that," Beowulf said, almost as if he'd been watching him all along. "Come, young warrior, and I will give you over to Ulfing, our master swordsman. Aelfhere," he said, turning to his friend and nodding at the messenger, "Hurthic here will take you to the quarters we reserve for honored guests."

"No sleeping bench in the king's mead hall?" Aelfhere asked with the ghost of a grin.

"There are some advantages to age," Beowulf said. "Hurthic, wine for the clan elder. And make sure he has his harp. There will be a banquet tonight!"

———

That was how it went, week after week. Arms training by day while the summer sun dozed a path through the sky, fine banquets by night with the skalds singing as the first precious mead of the season made its way around. As Beowulf had promised, Wiglaf sat on the most honored mead bench — not in the highest position, of course, but with warriors to the left and right of him that were twice his age and scarred with battle. When they received the king's gifts for raids and skirmishes, he always received something as well: a spiraling gold arm-ring, a saex only half as long as his sword but very sharp — "your weapon of last resort, boy," Ulfing told him — and his favorite gift of all, a hunting falcon he named Skritch. None of the other warriors seemed to mind that Wiglaf received a share of royal bounty even though he had never been to battle. "The king gives for what you will do, as well as for what you have done," the grizzled warrior to his right explained once. "It is how he knows we will always be loyal to him."

Wiglaf would have been loyal to Beowulf without any gifts at all, and told his grandfather so. "*You* would, Wiglaf," Aelfhere said, "but I have seen too many times the so-called loyalty of hearth companions."

The banquets were truly special for Wiglaf the nights Aelfhere sang his tales of Beowulf. The other skalds had little to compare with these except one old song that Wiglaf liked, mostly for its sadness. It told of an ancient and powerful clan that had completely died out, all but one lonely old man who was left with the clan's treasure, each piece sadly reminding him of the former owner. Eventually the old man found a secret barrow and buried all the treasure in it, then wandered, grieving, till his heart would bear no more. This would have been the end of the story except that a fire-breathing dragon discovered the barrow and decided to make it and its hoard his own. For three hundred years the dragon lay in the barrow, gloating over each item and counting all his treasures daily. Over the centuries the dragon grew until it nearly filled the barrow, and bits of gold and gems wedged themselves between its glittering green scales. The song made oath that the dragon and the hoard both truly existed somewhere, though no one knew where.

One night shortly after hearing the dragon song, Wiglaf had his first true seeing since leaving the Waegmunding clan house. He was readying himself for bed when it happened. His little sleeping chamber vanished, and he saw the Cape of the Whales shining in the moonlight. Just beyond the cliffs to the north there was a headland with what looked like a bite taken out of it high up the side of the sea face. From below, the bite could not be seen for all the rocks, but from above, if you leaned outward and looked down, the surprisingly flat, chalk-white bottom of the bite was plain to see between the cliffside and a huge boulder teetering over the sea. A faint trail led from the top of the headland to this strangely level place where a stream flowed out of darkness.

Wiglaf walked his vision trail to the stream winding its way soundlessly across the level before tumbling in a moon-glittered spume to the sea far below. He knelt to drink, but the water was hot. He spat it out, then, still kneeling, lifted his eyes to the darkness from which the stream came.

A man came out. He was moving quickly and breathing hard; a gorgeous goblet was in his hand. "I know you," Wiglaf said in his mind. "You are slave to Hethcyn, one of Beowulf's thanes." Of course the man paid him no heed, merely sent a panicked look over his shoulder at the cave he'd just left, then as good as galloped up the moonlit trail to the high moors.

Full of dread, Wiglaf got to his feet and moved toward the entrance of the cave. A sulfurous smoke puffed out at him, mingled with a rankness that made him gag. But he had to go on. The vision gave him no choice.

Inside the cave, Wiglaf let his eyes adjust. Finally he saw the outline of a huge, knobbly head lit redly by its own puffing nostrils. It was a

dragon, sound asleep. A dragon! And that slave had stolen something from it!

"There will be deaths to pay here," Wiglaf said, and he came free of his vision, saying it. Hugging himself tightly against the cold and the terror of his pounding heart, he tried to think. Had it already happened? Had the dragon wakened and missed its cup? Or was it all still to come?

A dragon in Geatland! But maybe it would not notice it had been robbed. Maybe it would not smell that there had been a man in its barrow.

Wiglaf closed his eyes and tried not to think how it would feel to burn to death. And that was when the dragon came.

———

Afterward the people who survived tried to describe what had happened. "He came like flying fire," one said, "and the thatch and the meadows flew burning behind him." Another, "Frecth's steading exploded in flames and his family, all afire, ran down the lane. We rolled them in blankets, but they died, they all died. And we, a thousand paces away, escaped completely." Another, "The dragon breathed death, and the horses screamed."

But after Wiglaf told about the true dream, it was what Aelfhere said that people always remembered. "Three hundred years the dragon has lived among us and we knew him not. Three hundred years he has brooded in the dark. And then someone came, walked insolently on the pillow he slept on, stole from him. And so this brooder in the dark vomited his rage on all the land, and it was the burning rage of one who has been forgotten and disrespected and owns only one small, glittering, dead place of his own that finally man has violated. We all, even dragons, have our limits."

Beowulf frowned. "He has killed many hundreds of my people, ruined their crops, wreaked havoc on their beasts and their dwellings."

"Oh, I do not say that he should continue to live," Aelfhere said quietly.

They called for Hethcyn and his slave. They heard how the slave had run away after a beating, then found shelter in the barrow and stole the goblet to win back his master's favor.

"You have caused this catastrophe," Beowulf told the slave. "Your penalty is to lead us to the dragon's lair."

"Do not ask me to help in killing him, oh, king!"

Beowulf laughed scornfully. "I need no help from cowards and villains. In any case, I will take no one's help. I am king of this land the dragon has violated, and it is my duty to rid my people of this enemy."

"Not alone, Beowulf!" Aelfhere cried.

"Do you question my duty, or my ability?"

They exchanged looks like swords, then Aelfhere shook his head. "Always alone, always. You have fought trolls weaponless and won; you have crushed enemies on the battlefield by your grip alone; you have swum league upon league weighed down by armor and weapons. You have nothing left to prove, Beowulf. And now you are old —"

"I fight this dragon alone," Beowulf interrupted. "I will take the warriors of my honored mead bench with me, but to watch only, just in case."

Wiglaf's heart thudded. He sat on the honored mead bench. But always when the others had gone raiding he had been kept at home. "I would come, too, sir," he said to Beowulf. "Please, sir. I would come."

"No, Wiglaf!" Aelfhere flashed. "Be quiet!"

"He is not too young to watch, Aelfhere," the king said.

"Always the same. Always you want witnesses."

"You are wrong, kinsman. The king *must* fight to defend his people. He must command no one to do what he would not."

"Let some of the better fighters help you at least —"

"The dragon is large, Aelfhere. The space Wiglaf described outside its lair is not. I will fight. The others will watch and see."

Aelfhere stared at him silently for a moment. "You will die, Beowulf," he said. "I read it in your thoughts. You believe that you will die."

Beowulf raised his chin. "What Fate chooses for us is not always what we believe. And if I should die, what better way than in warrior's harness, fighting an enemy of my people?"

"Leave Wiglaf home. Beowulf, please."

"He is of my honored mead bench. He chooses to come."

Aelfhere cast an appealing glance at Wiglaf.

"I am sorry, Grandfather," Wiglaf whispered.

"You will make of me something like that old man, last of his own kin, whose hoard-burial started this all. Eh, then, it will make a good song. Only it will not be I who will have the making of it." And Aelfhere turned, his hand pressed to his heart, and left the meeting chamber.

"I will need a body shield made all of iron," Beowulf said into the silence. "And my heirloom sword Naegling must be sharpened. Not with my grip alone can I destroy a fire-breathing dragon whose bite is certainly poisoned."

They left on horseback as soon as all was ready. There were thirteen of them, all armed and armored except for the thief, who led the way. It was a grim journey. They rode past steadings, roofless and worse; through forests still smoldering; up blackened hills where no bees hummed; and finally over rolling moors edged by sea cliffs. The Cape of the Whales was behind; to their left, the Eagle Cliffs; a short distance eastward a wooded knoll that had somehow escaped the dragon's wrath.

"He will hear the horses if we go farther," the thief said, waving his hand nervously at a tumble of rocks near the edge of the cliff. Beowulf looked to Wiglaf, who nodded. All but the thief dismounted.

"Return the horse to your master," Beowulf ordered him. "I have told Hethcyn not to harm you unduly." The scoundrel bolted at once.

"Lead the other horses there," Beowulf commanded, pointing eastward to the woody hill. One of his men began to obey, but for a long moment Beowulf wouldn't let go of his own white mount, the descendant of the champion King Hrothgar had given him so long ago. "Faithful Entaril," he said, "I am minded of your great sire today. Killing trolls gained me him, Entaril, and the saddle you bear so proudly was his. Oh, many struggles have I striven, many griefs of youth borne, even to my seventh winter watching my grandfather die of unavengeable sorrow that his second son by accident killed his first. Eh, eh, the obligations we must suffer for our honor! Go, Entaril, and safety take you. If I die may green pastures be yours."

Wiglaf watched, a lump in his throat, as Beowulf gave a last rub of the ears to the white stallion before it was taken away. He knew that Aelfhere had been right. Beowulf expected this fight to be his last.

"Warriors are with you, sir," Wiglaf got out, more loudly than he had intended. "You are not alone. Let us fight with you, as many as can fit by your side."

"No, no, Wiglaf. All of you, stay by the rock pile and watch. This is no fight against invading armies or raiders after our best sheep. Only I, the chief protector of this land, am obliged to fight this peril."

"But we may *choose* to fight without —" Wiglaf began, but one of the other men elbowed him to silence.

And so it was that Beowulf, gray in years and armor, went alone down the winding path to the chalky level outside the dragon's cave. There, stern and loud he shouted his summons, an honorable king seeking his Fate.

———

Red fire belched from the mouth of the cave. Beowulf's iron body shield glowed. He banged his sword hilt loudly against the inside. "Come out, Wyrm! You have killed my people. Now I will kill you!"

A knobbly head quested its way out of the cave. The mouth was drawn back in a kind of grin over sawblade teeth. To Wiglaf the slow exit from the cave seemed insolent, but Beowulf only stood still, watching.

Finally the red eyes appeared, hugely separated, one on either side of the scaled nose which was nearly as broad as the cave was high. From one side to the other the dragon swung his head, mouth open and dripping, letting both eyes see the king. Wiglaf understood then that Beowulf had been only waiting for those eyes to come within reach, so that he might plunge his sword Naegling into one of them. With scales everywhere else the eyes seemed the only paths into the dragon's life force.

Yes! Swift as a dancer Beowulf made a dash with Naegling across the chalky flat toward the right side of the dragon's head. He aimed for the eye, but the dragon tossed his head at the last moment and the blow missed. There was a ring as Naegling's point turned on bone, and a trumpet of fury from the dragon. More of him came out of the cave, fast now, very fast: huge shoulders that brushed both sides of the cave walls, leathery wings bent backward, bone to ground. One of the wings rammed Beowulf's shield. He stumbled backward, but did not quite fall. The dragon's chest emerged from the cave, and Wiglaf saw it enlarge. He shrieked. "He's going to breathe fire again! Beowulf, get back!"

Perhaps Beowulf heard. More likely he, too, saw his peril. Hastily he retreated back toward the cliffside. The dragon's massive head turned and reared up over the king, and coil upon coil of the rest of the body now poured out until it seemed that a roaring river of scales filled all the space in front of the cave. Yet still there was more of the body to come and nowhere for it to go, because in his rage the dragon had pinned his own wings to his sides and he could not take flight. And so the body emptied itself into itself, muscles contracting here and

expanding there until the wyrm's head was nearly as wide across as he was high. Beowulf halted with his back against the cliff, and now only the iron shield stood between him and certain death.

It was then that the dragon breathed. This time the blaze of fire was too hot to be merely red, but a terrible metallic yellow-streaked orange with the central blue of a smith's forge and a terrifying heart of whiteness. To Wiglaf, watching in horror even as he choked on the stink of sulfur, it seemed the blazing breath came from a spot so low down in the dragon's belly that it had leagues to go before it emerged, a distance that made the resulting flame seem to last forever and ever. And Beowulf was in the middle of it, enduring, enduring, his shield burning red, his helmet on fire, his gloved hand holding Naegling aflame, and Naegling itself as red as a brand from hell.

"We must help our lord!" Wiglaf cried to his hearth companions, the battle-scarred veterans who had sat with him so often on the mead bench.

But to a man they refused. "He said it was not our fight. He said we were to watch only."

"He said that so we would not be forced to fight. But we can *choose* to do so. And we must! Think of Beowulf's gifts to you. Think how often you swore your allegiance to him. Come, bring your swords to his aid!"

"Disobey our king? Never!"

Wiglaf choked back a sob. "And when he dies, and the dragon lives, whose fight will it be then?"

They turned on their heels and ran for the woods.

"There is only me," Wiglaf said then, and they were the loneliest words in the world. He looked once more down on his lord, an old man engulfed in his Fate. Then Wiglaf drew his own sword, that mighty blade of royal lineage that he had never used against living enemy, and without another wasted moment he sprang onto the track leading to hell.

Beowulf's movements were slow and clearly agony to him as he tried to ready himself for the dragon's next flame. "Hold on, dear lord," Wiglaf shouted. "I will help you."

Beowulf turned his head to Wiglaf behind the iron shield, and he smiled with a kind of joy. "Then there is not only me?" the king said. "For love, kinsman, you will aid me?" His words came very clearly. Behind his shield Wiglaf wept, but then the dragon was flaming again, and at the last moment he sent the blaze Wiglaf's way, so that his linden

shield turned instantly to ash, and the tears dried to salt on his burning cheeks, and the skin shriveled on the hand holding his heirloom sword.

"Quick, Wiglaf, behind me! My shield must do for us both!" Beowulf shouted.

The dragon was an unreal mass blurred by heat waves. But the red-hot iron of Beowulf's shield stood out, and Wiglaf jumped behind it. The dragon's tail came round to lash at him, but Beowulf stabbed at it with Naegling, and for once the blade penetrated. It was no mortal wound, but the greasy blood boiled out and the dragon's head came downward in pain. Then, with a speed so swift Wiglaf could only gape at it, the king leaped up and struck with the strength of thirty men — thirty young men! — at the dragon's skull.

It was a blow that would have penetrated the magic corselets of the dwarfs, had the sword been able to bear it. But always there is a Curse for a Gift, and this was Beowulf's, that in the end he was too strong for his own weapons, even Naegling. And so, instead of killing the dragon as it should, faithful Naegling shattered. The dragon reeled for a moment only, then shook off the pain and dropped his head still further, clawing away the shield and opening his enormous mouth to bite Beowulf's head off. At the same moment Beowulf lunged forward to butt the drag-on with his forehead, so that instead of closing around Beowulf's neck, the poisoned fangs only raked at the exposed part of Beowulf's face. And then he began to take breath to flame again.

Wiglaf had been training for only one summer in the arts of warfare. He had seen only fourteen winters and listened to steading tales for only ten of those, and none had been about how to kill a dragon. But he knew about animals, and he had observed what happened when the dragon flamed before. And so as the dragon prepared for what would certainly be his final attack, Wiglaf looked only for that spot in the lower belly, the place where the furnace must be, and he watched and waited until the dragon's breath reached it, widening the belly there so that the scales parted a little, just a very little.

Quick, Wiglaf told himself, do it before the air inside turns to fire! One boy and one sword and one thrust only to stop the terrible thing that was about to happen. And Wiglaf leaped forward and with all the strength and weight he could muster he plunged his shining blade hilt-deep into that precise spot in the dragon's lower belly, between the scales, deep into the furnace that made the dragon's fire.

The dragon gasped. The blaze failed. Bewildered and in pain the dragon arched backward, parting the scales of his belly still more. And Beowulf, poisoned and bleeding and burned almost past belief, took his razor-sharp saex from his belt and joined it with his warrior's training and his Waegmunding Gift in both his hands. And the blade sang as he swung it at the monster's belly, and Wiglaf thought his heart had stopped or time had stopped or maybe the world, because instead of destroying Beowulf and himself and the entire Geat kingdom, the dragon fell dead, cloven in two by a mere saex in a king's dying hands.

"For our people, Wiglaf!" Beowulf roared. "We have killed him together, you and I, we two alone in all the world."

Wiglaf shook. The dragon was dead. He had helped kill him. The dragon was dead. Tears filled his eyes.

Mastering himself, he turned to Beowulf, who was moving very slowly and carefully to a flat boulder. With a shock of horror Wiglaf saw now the blood on Beowulf's face, swollen and oozing from the poison of the dragon's teeth. The king sat down, heavily, not on the stone but in front of it, leaning back on it and gazing out at the sea. He did not look at the dragon. He did not even seem to see Wiglaf.

"Beowulf?" Wiglaf called. "My lord?" There was no reply. Here on this desolate cliff there were no healing herbs. There was nothing at all that might help with the poison. But if the poison could only be diluted, perhaps there was a chance.

Wiglaf leaped from coil to coil of the dragon to the stream that exited the cave. There was a goblet stuck between two of the dragon's scales. He yanked it free, filled it with lukewarm water and hurried back, damning the dragon's bulk that even dead seemed determined to trip him up.

At Beowulf's side he said tremblingly, "Sir, I am going to cleanse your face." Beowulf didn't move or speak. Gently Wiglaf poured the water little by little on the ragged, gaping wounds.

Fresh blood mingled with the old, pouring in a split red stream to the ground. The king flinched. "Ah, my lord, I am sorry. I am trying to take away some of the poison."

"My thanks for your kindness," Beowulf said very slowly. "But the poison is deep within me. There is nothing anyone can do."

"You're not going to...oh, lord, please don't —" Wiglaf stopped before he wept.

"Neh, neh, boy. Death is no terrible thing for one who has lived well. For fifty winters I cared for my people, and they lived in peace. Feuds I never sought, nor did I falsely swear any oath, and I always did my best with whatever situation Fate sent me. As a king, I will die well. I have been lucky in Aelfhere, and more lucky than I deserve in you." He paused, breathing shallowly and fast. "The water hurts just a little, but it is cool, too, against the burning. And I would be clean, ere I die."

Wiglaf nodded, and now he could not hold back the tears. Slowly, carefully, he took off Beowulf's boar helmet. He poured the rest of the water over Beowulf's head, then ran again to refill it.

"The collar, warrior," Beowulf managed, when he returned.

Wiglaf undid the hinge at the back, then opened it as wide as possible before taking it off from the front. Beowulf gave a gasp that would have been a groan in any lesser man. I must make him clean, Wiglaf told himself, holding onto the thought with all his might. I must make him clean.

He did his best, ripping cloth from the tunic he wore under his father's corselet and binding the strips gently around Beowulf's neck. Sometime during that task Beowulf fainted, and Wiglaf was glad of it and afraid at the same time. "You are not yet clean, lord," he got out between sobs. "Please don't die yet." Then he cleansed the silk-silver rings of the heirloom mail corselet that Wayland Smith had forged in the time of the gods.

Beowulf woke then, his eyes feverish. "That is better," he said, gazing at the gold collar Wiglaf had washed and placed in his corseleted lap along with the ring. He gave Wiglaf a gentle look. "You have been burned, too, warrior. Do not waste all your water on me."

"I...must...make...you...clean."

"And so I am, thanks to you. Wiglaf..."

"My lord?"

Beowulf fingered the collar of kingship in his lap. "I have no heir. You are my only close kin, you and Aelfhere. And Aelfhere is too old and too cranky to be king." With a mighty effort the old king held out his golden collar. "Wiglaf son of Weohstan, take you the collar of kingship from me. I bid you, King of the Geats, to care for your people as you have cared for me today."

The voice, the eyes, the words were magical. Wiglaf could not have stopped himself from taking the collar if he tried. Trembling, he put it around his own neck. I am to be king, he told himself. King! "Please, Beowulf, I am too young," he said, even as he fastened the latch at the back.

"Aelfhere will help you, and your mead bench will also. Not all honor guards are cowardly and love not their lord. Aelfhere knows good men from bad. He will not let you promote men as I did."

"They are back from their flight," Wiglaf said reluctantly. "They're up there on the cliff top right now. Some of them called to me to ask how you were."

"Yes, now that they know the dragon's dead. You did not answer?"

"No. They deserve nothing from either of us."

"Wiglaf son of Weohstan, you have taken the collar of kingship. Swear that you will not punish my false companions unduly. People cannot be made to love their lords. The fault here must be as much mine as theirs."

"They can be shamed, though, for loving their own skins more than their duty," Wiglaf said fiercely. "And that I will certainly do."

Beowulf looked at him oddly. "Well, you are the king," he said at last. Then he gave Wiglaf the jeweled ring and helmet, and told him to take the magic corselet later. "Time runs quickly from my veins," he said then. "And yet I have a mind to see the hoard that you and I have made ours, now that the dragon is gone."

"I would not leave you, sir."

"I ask your mercy in this, King Wiglaf."

What could he do? Running, stumbling on coils of dead dragon, falling and running again, Wiglaf entered the dragon's cave. In the dusky light he saw piles of gems and rusty helmets, marvels of arm-rings and precious statues of ivory and jewels. There were so many treasures that he almost panicked. How could he take them all for Beowulf to see? In the end he grabbed up as many golden beakers and plates as his arms would hold, and one gloriously woven shining banner, and ran with them out of the cave to where Beowulf lay still, his eyes closed. "Sir. Sir! Oh, Beowulf, please..."

The old man opened his eyes, and those eyes smiled at Wiglaf, smiled at the treasure he bore in his arms. "Thus I may leave gifts for my people, thanks be to Fate. Kinsman, I would have you make a barrow for my ashes and place it on the seaward edge of the Cape of the Whales. That way mariners from over the sea will see Beowulf's barrow and remember my name."

"And know to avoid the hidden reefs there," Wiglaf said. "All people seeing it will know you cared for everyone, not just those who are your own."

Beowulf closed his eyes. His voice was so low Wiglaf had to bend over his lips to hear it. "Fate has swept almost all whom I have loved to the land of doom. I...would...follow them now."

His breath shuddered out. Wiglaf waited. Beowulf never breathed again.

———

So passed Beowulf, King of the Geats. There was work to be done, as there always is after a king's death. A public proclamation of the new monarch had to be made, and oaths of loyalty taken by all the thanes to the new king. The ten hearth companions who had abandoned Beowulf were publicly shamed; others were chosen for Wiglaf's protection and advice by Aelfhere, after he had read their thoughts carefully. A wagon was summoned to carry Beowulf's body and all the treasure from the dragon's lair to the top of the Cape of the Whales. From all over Geatland firewood came, wagons and people with their sticks of wood and their own small treasures. Beowulf's funeral pile was hung with helmets and weapons and other harness of war, and under his body were simple treasures from the common people who had benefited from half a century of his peace. And on a still, still morning with the nip of autumn in the air, they burned Beowulf. It was the biggest balefire in all the history of Geatland.

When the fire had burned away, Wiglaf ordered that all the treasure from the dragon's lair be placed amid Beowulf's ashes, where, he said, "It will be as useless to men as it always was." People obeyed his command and made no complaint, for he was king now, and had, as everyone knew, helped to slay the great dragon. Afterward, with Wiglaf as witness, they built a barrow of stone and turf over the ashes of Beowulf's body and all the treasure, and when it was done it towered high above the Cape of the Whales as Beowulf had wished. During the sunset after it was finished, Wiglaf and his new hearth companions rode around the barrow many times, chanting their dirge and doing honor to the dead king. They praised his leadership, his acts of might and courage, his love for his people, and the gratitude they owed to him.

"Of men he was the mildest and most generous," sang Wiglaf with

the rest. "To his kin he was the kindest, and more than any other king, he was keenest for praise."

Aelfhere did not sing. Many skalds and later bards made stories of Beowulf and his fight with the dragon, but never Aelfhere. Of the ending of Beowulf, these were the only words that Aelfhere ever said:

"You should know, oh, Geats, that when a man looks for praise, it is often love that he truly seeks."

When people heard these words they did not understand. Beowulf of the Geats had been a great king and a great man. He had always had their love.

Always.

AUTHOR'S NOTE

The story *Beowulf* was sung by bards (or "skalds") for at least two hundred years before it was first written down. The oldest known written version of the story is an epic poem that comes from the eighth century A.D. and is in the West Saxon language.

The events in *Beowulf* took place in a small area between the North Sea and the Baltic Sea. The Geats (King Hygelac's people who were later ruled by his nephew, Beowulf) probably lived near the modern coastal village of Fjällbacka in an area of Sweden between Göteborg and Oslo in Norway. Heorot (the hall of the Danish King Hrothgar) was likely at Gamie Leire near Roskilde on the island of Zealand (which is now part of Denmark). Historical sources tell us that Hygelac was killed in a battle in A.D. 521. From this we can guess that other events of *Beowulf*, if indeed any of them are true, would have taken place roughly between A.D. 500 and A.D. 571.

From more than a dozen English translations of the original poem that I read in both verse and prose, there were six* that I referred to again and again in order to keep my version of *Beowulf* an honest rendition of the original story (sticking to the "truth" where those six translations told me what the truth was and making up only a few things that were not in the original poem but might have happened).

To see what other people had done in retelling the legend (rather than directly translating it), I also read Rosemary Sutcliff's *Beowulf*, *The Heroic Deeds of Beowulf* by Gladys Schmitt, and *Beowulf: A Likeness* by Randolph Swearer, Raymond Oliver, Marijane Osborn (Contributor) and Fred C. Robinson. Wiglaf was always mentioned (if at all) only at the end of the story, where (as in the translations) he is the youngest of Beowulf's mead-bench warriors and the only one to come to his aid against the dragon. However, Wiglaf was named as a Waegmunding, as was Aelfhere, and they were related to Beowulf through the Waegmunding line. It seemed to me possible that Beowulf's supernatural gifts (the strength of thirty men, his being able to hold his breath for hours underwater) might reflect a genetic "kink" of the Waegmundings — that they were all gifted with different kinds of supernatural talents. No one that I know of has ever postulated this before, but none of the translations say it couldn't have happened. The Waegmunding gift that I made up made it possible for me to tell the story through the eyes of Wiglaf, something I really wanted to do in a book for a young audience. — W W K

*Translations by Francis B. Gummere (Macmillan, 1909), Kevin Crossley-Holland (Macmillan, 1968), Stanley B. Greenfield (*Readable Beowulf*, Southern Illinois University Press, 1982, with a fascinating introduction by Alain Renoir), David Wright (Penguin, 1957), Albert W. Haley Jr. (Branden Press, 1978), and the widely studied E. Talbot Donaldson translation (W.W. Norton, 1975).

Text copyright © 1999 by Welwyn Wilton Katz
Illustrations copyright © 1999 by Laszlo Gal
Reprinted 2000

All rights reserved. No part of this book may be reproduced, stored in a retrieval system or transmitted in any form or by any means, without the prior written permission of the publisher or, in the case of photocopying or other reprographic copying, a licence from CANCOPY (Canadian Reprography Collective), Toronto, Ontario.

Groundwood Books / Douglas & McIntyre
720 Bathurst Street, Suite 500, Toronto, Ontario M5S 2R4

Distributed in the USA by Publishers Group West
1700 Fourth Street, Berkeley, CA 94710

We acknowledge the financial support of the Canada Council for the Arts, the Ontario Arts Council and the Government of Canada through the Book Publishing Industry Development Program for our publishing activities.

Canadian Cataloguing in Publication Data
Katz, Welwyn
Beowulf
"A Groundwood book".
ISBN 0-88899-365-X
1. Beowulf- Adaptations. I. Gal, Laszlo. II. Title.
PS8571.A889B46 1999   jC813'.54   C99-930265-5
PZ8.1.K154B4 1999

Printed and bound in China by Everbest Printing Co. Ltd.